Library of Congress Cataloging in Publication Data:
Elliott, Dan. Ernie's little lie. (Sesame Street start-to-read books) SUMMARY: Ernie enters a painting
by his cousin Fred in a contest in order to win a box of paints.
  [1. Honesty—Fiction. 2. Painting—Fiction. 3. Puppets—Fiction] I. Mathieu, Joseph, ill.
II. Title. III. Series. PZ7.E446Er [E] 82-7574 AACR2 ISBN: 0-394-85440-3 (trade);
0-394-95440-8 (lib. bdg.) Manufactured in the United States of America   2 3 4 5 6 7 8 9 0

A Sesame Street Start-to-Read Book™

Ernie's Little Lie

by Dan Elliott•illustrated by Joe Mathieu

Featuring Jim Henson's Sesame Street Muppets

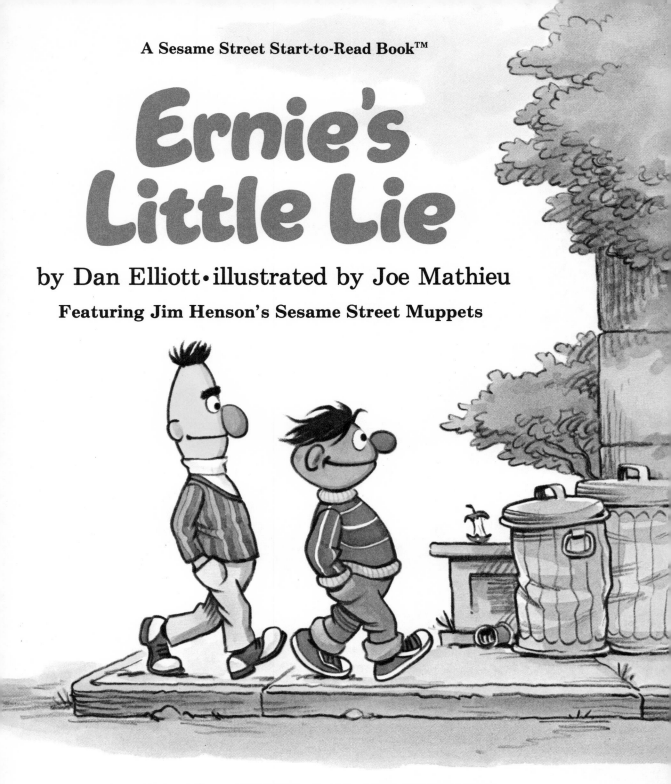

Random House/Children's Television Workshop

One day Ernie and Bert
were walking by
Mister Hooper's store.
Suddenly Ernie stopped.
"Look at that!" he said.

Ernie pressed his nose
to the store window.
Inside was a beautiful box
of paints. It had lots of
colors—even gold and silver.
"Gee," said Ernie. "I wish
I had that box of paints."

ART
CONTEST
PRIZE!
THIS PAINT SET

"Maybe you can have it," said Bert.
"Mister Hooper is having a contest.
The painter of the best picture
wins that box of paints."

Ernie started to run home.
"Wow!" he said. "I am going
to paint a picture right now!"

Ernie got out his old paint box.

Then he got some paper.

He was ready to start painting.

The doorbell rang.

"I have a letter for you, Ernie,"
   said the mailman.
"Thanks," said Ernie.
   Then he said good-bye
   to the mailman
   and opened his letter.

The letter was from his cousin.

It said:

Dear Ernie,
I painted a picture for you.
I hope you like it!
Love, Cousin Fred

It was a great picture of a tiger.
"Wow!" said Ernie.
"It is so much better than
any of my pictures."
And then Ernie got an idea.

"What if I told Mister Hooper
that I painted this tiger?
Then I would be sure to win
the contest," said Ernie.

Ernie's heart beat faster.

He looked at the painting again.

"No, I cannot lie," he said.

Ernie hung the tiger painting
on the wall.
"Now I will paint my own picture
for the contest," he said.

He painted a picture
of Rubber Duckie.
It was a good painting.

Bert saw the tiger painting
as soon as he came home.
"What a great painting!"
he said. "You will win the
contest for sure, old buddy!"

He took the painting off the wall.
"I'll take it to Mister Hooper
for you," said Bert happily.
"Wait, Bert," said Ernie.
"There is something I have
to tell you."
"Tell me later," Bert said.
SLAM went the door.

Ernie looked sadly at his
painting of Rubber Duckie.
He rolled it up
and put it in his pocket.

Then he put on his sneakers
and went outside.
"I must tell Mister Hooper
the truth," he said.

But before Ernie got to
Mister Hooper's store,
Big Bird saw him.

"Ernie!" shouted Big Bird.
"Your tiger painting is great!
I bet it will win the contest."
"Do you really think so?"
asked Ernie.

"Yes, I do," said Big Bird.
"And so does everyone else.
  Don't be late for the contest."
  And Big Bird ran off.

But Ernie just sat on the curb.
"I want that paint box,"
 he said softly.
"But I don't want to lie.
 How did I get into this mess?"

At last Ernie went to the store.
Everyone was already there,
and everyone had a painting.

Bert's was a broom.

Oscar's was a garbage can.

Big Bird's was a big sunflower.

But the best painting of all

was the tiger.

"All of these paintings are good,"
said Mister Hooper.
"But only one person can win.
First prize goes to...
ERNIE!"

Mister Hooper gave Ernie
the beautiful box of paints,
and everyone clapped.
"Thank you," Ernie said sadly.

Then Big Bird said,
"Ernie, may I have your painting
to hang by my nest?"
Ernie looked at Big Bird
and burst into tears.

"I did not paint that tiger!"
he cried.
"My cousin painted it."
He took out his picture
of Rubber Duckie.
"This is my painting!"

"Ernie, so THAT'S what you wanted
to tell me!" said Bert.
"YES!" cried Ernie.
Bert put his arm around Ernie.

"It is not always easy
to tell the truth," said Bert.
"But you did it!
I'm proud of you, old buddy."

"I will mail the paint box
to my cousin," Ernie said.
"Because HE really won it."
Everyone cheered.

"You didn't win the contest,"
said Bert, "but you painted the
best picture ever of Rubber Duckie.
And that is no lie!"